CREAK! Said the Bed

For Bonnie Claire — welcome!
P. R.

To my wife, Debbie, and to Mom, Dad, Brandon, Jaimie,
Ed, Joyce, and my good friend Mr. Pickles
R. D.

First edition 2010

Library of Congress Cataloging-in-Publication Data.
Root, Phyllis.
Creak! said the bed / Phyllis Root ; illustrated by Regan Dunnick. — 1st ed.
p. cm.
Summary: In the middle of a dark, stormy night, one child, then another, then a third wake their mother
and ask to climb into the bed, but when the last member of the family arrives Papa declares there is no more room.
ISBN 978-0-7636-2004-2
[1. Stories in rhyme. 2. Beds — Fiction. 3. Sleep — Fiction. 4. Storms — Fiction.
5. Family life — Fiction. 6. Dogs — Fiction.] I. Dunnick, Regan, ill. II. Title.
PZ8.3.R667Cre 2010
[E] — dc22 2009022130

09 10 11 12 13 14 LEO 10 9 8 7 6 5 4 3 2 1

Printed in Heshan, Guangdong, China

This book was typeset in Kosmik.
The illustrations were done in acrylic gouache.

Candlewick Press
99 Dover Street
Somerville, Massachusetts 02144

visit us at www.candlewick.com

CREAK! Said the Bed

Phyllis Root

illustrated by Regan Dunnick

CANDLEWICK PRESS

One dark night in the middle of the night, Momma and Poppa were snoozing in bed.

SQUEAK, went the door.

And Evie said,

Poppa said, Snore,
and Momma said, "Sure!
There's plenty of room for Evie in the bed."

So Evie bounced in.

CREAK, said the bed.

That same night, that dark, cold night,
Momma and Poppa and Evie were snoozing in bed.
Squeak, went the door.
And Ivy said,

I'm freezing in my bed.
Can I come in with you?

Poppa said, **Snark,**
and Momma said, "Sure!
There's plenty of room for Ivy in the bed."

So Ivy plopped in.

CREAK, said the bed.

That same night, that dark, cold, windy night,

Momma and Poppa and Evie and Ivy were snoozing in bed.

Squeak, went the door.

And Mo said,

It's spooky in my room.
Can I come in with you?

Poppa said, **Snurkle,**

and Momma said, "Sure!

There's plenty of room for Mo in the bed."

So Mo squeezed in.

CREAK, said the bed.

That same night, that dark, cold, windy, rainy night,

Momma and Poppa and Evie and Ivy and Mo were all snoozing in bed. . . .

BOOM! went the thunder.

Clickety-clackity,
click-clack.

SQUEEEEEAK,
went the door.

"Woof!" said Fred.

Up Poppa popped.
Poppa cried, "**Stop!**
There's no more room for Fred in the bed."

But Fred leaped in.

CRACK,

said the bed.

SNOOF, said Fred. Momma and Evie and Ivy and Mo said, SNORE.

Poppa scratched his head
and Poppa said, "Guess there's plenty
of room for us all in the bed!"

One dark night in the middle of the night,
in the middle of the bed,
in the middle of the floor,
Poppa said, "Good night."

CREAK, said the floor.